You will find the names of the shapes
in this book.

In this book young children are introduced to the names of basic shapes and colors.

Each page is illustrated using bold, colorful pictures of objects within the range of a child's experience. The pages ask simple questions to promote discussion and practice is given in counting and color and shape recognition.

Available in Series S808

∗ a is for apple
I can count
Tell me the time
Colors and shapes
Nursery Rhymes

∗*Also available as* Ladybird Teaching Frieze

Colors and shapes

written by LYNNE BRADBURY

illustrated by LYNN N GRUNDY

Ladybird Books Loughborough

This shape is called a **circle**.
It goes round and round and round.
It has no corners.

A wheel is a **circle** shape.
How many wheels can you count
on this page?
Do you know some more **circle** shapes?

The color of this circle is called **red**.
There are lots of different **reds**.

Here are some **red** things.
Do you know what they are?

This shape is called a **square**.
It has four sides the same length
and four corners.

The windows on these houses
are **square** shapes.
How many windows does each house have?

The elephant has made this square
a color called **blue** .
There are many different **blues.**

Which things are **blue** on this page?

This shape is called a **triangle**.
It has three sides and three corners.

The three sides of a **triangle** need not be the same length.
Count how many **triangles** there are on this page.

The color of this triangle is called **yellow**.
There are different **yellows**.

Can you name these things?
What color are they?

Here is a shape called a **rectangle**.
It has four corners and four sides.
Two sides are long and two sides are short.

Rectangles can be long, short, fat or thin.
How many **rectangles** are there
on this page?
Which **rectangle** is yellow?

The boy is painting the rectangle **blue**.
The girl is painting it **yellow**.
Blue and **yellow** mixed together
make a color called **green**.
There are different greens.

What are these **green** things?

The monkeys have found some **red** paint and some **yellow** paint.
When they mix them together it makes a color called **orange**.

What have the monkeys painted **orange**?

The cat has some **blue** paint.
The dog has some **red** paint.
Red and **blue** mixed together
make a color called **purple**.

Name the shapes on this page.
Which shapes are colored **purple**?

Everything on these pages is
black and **white**.
The witch has a **black** cat.
The rabbit is **white**.

Talk about the **black** and **white** things.

If we mix some **black** and some **white**
it makes a color called **grey**.
What are these **grey** animals called?

If we mix a little bit of **red** with **white** it makes a color called **pink**.

What are these **pink** things?
Have you seen **pink** flowers?

Which colors in this rainbow do you know?